SAY  TO THE
DRESS

Keren David

Barrington Stoke

First published in 2022 in Great Britain by
Barrington Stoke Ltd
18 Walker Street, Edinburgh, EH3 7LP

www.barringtonstoke.co.uk

A CIP catalogue record for this book is available
from the British Library upon request

ISBN: 978-1-80090-087-5

Printed by Hussar Books, Poland

To Beverley

Chapter 1

The dress is bright red with black stripes – it's a jumper dress with a roll neck. It would look great with black tights and my lace-up boots.

That is, it would look great if anyone else was wearing it. Anyone apart from me.

"Just try it, Miri," says Sophie. She's my best friend. When we're older, she's determined to be a stylist. She's very determined. Sophie wants to work with celebrities, but until then she's practising on me. I'm not so keen on being dressed up – and I'm certainly no celebrity. But I love Sophie. I do it for her.

There's just one problem. The problem is me.

"The dress won't fit," I tell her. There's no way. Those skinny, stripy arms, that tiny skirt …

"It's stretchy! It's jersey! It's body-con!" Sophie says.

Body-con stands for body-confident or body-contouring or body-conditioning – I can never remember which. It basically means that the clothes will cling to every bit of your body. But I am not feeling confident or conditioned. My contours are like a mountain range. My body has betrayed me lately.

One year ago I was a small and skinny and flat-chested thirteen year old. No one ever looked at me. I was fast on my feet, good at netball and gymnastics. I liked my body. Mum and Alice, my older sister, were both slender and sporty, so I was sure that was how I was going to stay.

But then things happened. Things that made me less sure, less confident. Along came puberty. Hello, spots. Hello, massive breasts that jiggle around if I run. Which meant goodbye, sporting career. Hello, sweaty patches under my arms. Oh, and I'm about six inches taller – taller than Mum, taller than Alice, and nearly as tall as Dad and my brother, Adam.

I've also got wider. And bits of my body have taken on a life of their own. Yes, gigantic, spotty bum, I'm talking about you.

Plus I got Covid, and then Long Covid, which meant months of not seeing anyone. I didn't do anything very much apart from feel miserable and eat flapjacks and watch daytime TV. I watched a lot of *Embarrassing Bodies*. I binged *Come Dine with Me*. I even got a bit addicted to *Say Yes to the Dress*.

Getting bigger meant I had to have a completely new school uniform when I finally went back to school. "Ho, ho, ho, it's the jolly green giant!" my dad said to me when he first saw me in it. This made me hate him, and hate myself, and especially hate whoever it was that decided our skirts and blazers would be a disgusting shade of "forest green".

"Dad's just trying to cheer you up, Miri," said Mum. "You know his jokes are rubbish." That didn't help at all.

None of my clothes fit any more. And none of the hand-me-downs from Alice fit either. And today, none of the clothes that Sophie has ordered from Depop have fit me. Which is a shame

3

because Sophie's plan was to let me pick my favourite as my birthday present.

"I don't like body-con," I tell Sophie. But I agree to try the jumper dress. I pull it on over my big fat head. I tug it over my gigantic bouncing chest. I thrust one arm into a sleeve ...

And I am completely stuck. I can't see a thing.

"Help!" I squeak in a tiny, muffled voice.

Ding dong! Sophie's front door rings. And rings again. *Ding dong, ding dong, ding dong.*

"Hang on!" says Sophie. I think she means she's going to help me, but then I hear the bedroom door creak and I realise she's answering the front door first.

Gah! I wriggle and twist and push and pull and ... Am I going to die by dress? Will I ever see the light of day again? I try to pull it over my shoulders and there's a massive ripping noise ...

"Oh my god, Miri! What have you done?"

I know that voice. That's not Sophie.

"I can't believe you tried that on!"

It's Toxic Tiffany. Now I'm definitely going to die.

"I could have told you it wouldn't fit!" Tiffany goes on. "What are you going to do now?"

Unbelievable. I have ruined a brand-new dress in front of my arch-enemy. And I am still stuck in it, head and shoulders cocooned, gigantic bum on show.

"What a disaster!" says Toxic Tiffany. I suspect she's trying not to laugh.

"Are you all right, Miri?" says Sophie.

"Yes," I say in a faint voice, struggling with the dress. "I'm fine!"

But of course I mean no. I'm not fine at all.

Chapter 2

Toxic Tiffany was in my class at primary school. She was a general pain there, always hogging the school hamster, saying, "He loves me better than all of you!" and showing off about her handwriting skills. She swapped best friends every year. There was always some massive drama in which Tiffany's feelings were hurt or someone was bullying her or something was "so unfair". I kept my distance.

I thought I'd got rid of Toxic Tiffany when we went to secondary school and were put in different forms. I sat next to Sophie on the first day and knew I'd found a soulmate. But last year Tiffany and Sophie were in the same group for their Textiles class, and they bonded over a shared love of fashion. They were constantly messaging each other with pictures of "designer" this and "vintage" whatever.

And now Sophie keeps trying to persuade me that Tiffany's really nice and not toxic at all. Fat chance.

With their help, I wrestle my way out of the body-con dress from hell. I emerge flushed, sweaty and trying hard not to cry.

"Promise me you didn't take any pictures!" I demand.

"Of course we didn't," says Sophie, while Tiffany smirks.

I check their phones to make sure. OK, they didn't – but I bet Tiffany wanted to.

"It was my fault," says Sophie. "That dress didn't have as much give as I'd thought ..."

"You can't blame yourself," says Tiffany. "Every fabric has its limits." Ugh, she's so annoying.

I get back in my own personal comfort zone – leggings, a huge black jumper and trainers. I blink away the tears. After all, I have only myself to blame.

"Well, thanks a lot," I say.

"Can I try the dress?" asks Tiff. She disappears to the bathroom with the horror frock.

"What's she doing here?" I hiss at Sophie. "Why didn't you warn me?"

"Oh, Miri, she's not so bad," Sophie says. "And she really wanted to see you. Said she had something to ask you."

"Ta da!" Tiffany says, appearing again.

Naturally the dress looks great on Tiff. It clings to her curves and makes her waist look tiny and her legs super long. She walks up and down Sophie's room like she's on a catwalk.

"I think I can mend the bit where you ripped it, Miri," Tiff says. "No one will notice."

"Oh, good," says Sophie. "Because I can't send it back now it's torn. You have it, Tiff."

Tiffany blows her a kiss. "Can I really, Soph? You're so lovely!"

"Anyway, I think I might get going," I say. "I've got to help get the barbecue ready."

"I'll get you something different for your birthday," says Sophie. "It's a shame none of these dresses worked ... but I'll find something. Maybe an accessory. Handbags are always good. Or a scarf or something."

"Don't worry about my birthday," I tell Sophie.

"You must be super excited for the barbecue," Sophie says. "Is everyone coming?"

"Everyone!" I reply. "Alice is coming from Manchester, and Adam—"

"Adam?" says Tiffany. "So you have a brother called Adam McVitie?"

"Yes ... my half-brother," I say, to be completely accurate.

"I don't remember you having brothers and sisters at school," Tiffany says. "I thought you were a lonely old only child."

"Like me!" says Sophie. "Miri's so lucky," she goes on. "With a sister and brother who are loads older than she is. Like totally grown-ups."

"Half-sister and half-brother," I say. Personally, I think it would be more fun to have siblings that weren't a lot older than you. And also it would be nice if they didn't have family that aren't related to you, but there you go. I love Alice and Adam hugely, and they love me, so I'm not complaining.

"Yeah, whatever," says Sophie.

"Why are you asking about Adam?" I say to Tiffany.

"It isn't really a common name," she says. "Except for the biscuits. Are you related to them?"

My surname means I've been hearing old rubbish jokes about McVitie's digestives since I was in primary school. I'm sure Tiffany must remember the jokes from back then, so I shoot her a look to kill and say, "No."

"I wish I had older brothers and sisters," says Sophie. "Or any brothers or sisters. You are both so lucky."

"Thanks, hun," says Tiffany. "It is amazing getting all the hand-me-downs from my sisters."

I remember Tiffany's sisters from primary school. Scarlett and Lola and Lily. All tall and blonde and blue eyed. Always the princesses in the school plays. Always the netball captains.

Always the ones chosen to give a bunch of flowers to special guests.

"So, why were you asking about Adam?" I say again.

Tiff giggles and says, "Well, it's just that Scarlett has a new boyfriend. A handsome banker. And his name is Adam McVitie, so I just wondered if he was any relation of yours. But they met in Edinburgh, and that's probably crawling with people called McVitie, so don't worry! Although just imagine if it was your brother and my sister ..."

"Half-brother," I say automatically. Inside, my stomach is churning. Surely Adam wouldn't ... would he?

But Adam does live in Edinburgh, and he works for a bank. And Scarlett was so pretty, even at school, years older than me. She must be about 21 now. Adam's 25 ... It must be ... It can't be ...

"Just think if they got married!" says Toxic Tiff. "We could be joint bridesmaids! Imagine!"

"Amazing!" says Sophie.

No, I think. *No, please, no*. That's not a good thought at all.

Chapter 3

When I get home, my sister Alice has arrived for my birthday barbecue. We hug, and I try not to mind that she's so dainty and fine-boned and pretty. Hugging Alice makes my body feel even more squishy and awkward and big.

"You've got so tall!" Alice says, which makes me feel like an elephant towering over a fluffy bunny. I'd better be careful not to crush her under my massive lumbering feet. I can almost feel my nose expand to the size of a trunk.

"Not really," I mumble, hunching my shoulders and ducking my head. Alice and Mum are chopping vegetables for salads and dips, so I grab a knife and sit down at the table and get to work. Together we cut cucumber and tomatoes. I mix oil and vinegar, mustard and sugar to make my special salad dressing. Dad is in the garden, setting up the barbecue. Mum puts a pan of potatoes on to boil and dices pickled cucumbers for her signature potato salad.

"Are you going to get changed?" Mum asks me.

Into what? I think. "I wasn't going to, no," I say.

"I just thought you might put on a nice skirt or something," Mum adds.

I give her an eyeroll. "I don't like skirts!" I say. "I don't have anything like that! I'm fine like this!"

"It's just ... you're always in leggings. I thought you might want to dress up a bit?"

"No thanks," I snarl. And then I feel a bit guilty because Mum's going to all this trouble for my birthday.

"You look great as you are," says Alice, and I'm grateful to her. She and Mum both look lovely in floaty sundresses. Mum's is bright pink; Alice is in sunset orange. It's like I'm a totally different species in my black jumper.

"How's life?" I ask Alice, expecting the usual.

Alice is a junior doctor, so her life is all work, work, work. Last year she was working in accident and emergency, so it was scary and stressful. Now Alice has moved on to a children's ward, so I'm waiting for stories about toddlers with cancer. You know, cheery stuff like that.

But instead Alice blushes and says, "It's all good actually."

"It is?" says Mum, dropping her knife in amazement.

"Really?" I ask.

"Yes, really good," Alice says. A goofy smile spreads over her face, which is funny to see because Alice has one of those faces that just looks serious most of the time. A long straight nose, pointed chin, dark eyes.

"Have you … met someone?" asks Mum.

I splutter and say, "Don't be silly! Alice has no time for meeting anyone! And she's not interested in falling in love or getting married or anything like that! She's said so a million times!"

But Alice is shaking her head. "You're wrong, Miri. I have actually met someone. And he's so lovely."

"Who? When?" I demand.

"How? Who?" says Mum at exactly the same time.

"He's called Jacob," Alice says. "We met a few months ago at Grandma and Grandpa's house. His parents are friends of theirs."

The grandparents that Alice is talking about aren't the same as the grandma that we share. That's Mum's mum, who insists we call her Sadie and is water-skiing in Greece right now. Alice's other grandparents are called Joe and Betty Goldstein. They live in Manchester, near where she works, and they totally adore her. Partly because she's Alice, and partly because she reminds them of Alice's dad, who died when Alice was two.

Mum never really talks about how hard it was having a husband who got ill with cancer just after their baby was born. He died a year later. "I don't like to dwell on sad times," Mum says if I ask. But I know that Alice decided to be a doctor because she wants to help people who get ill like her dad did. I know that she's very close to his parents and spends the Jewish festivals with them every year.

It's kind of sad for us that Alice is never here for the Jewish festivals. But it's also kind of easier because Dad and Adam aren't Jewish at all, and Mum and I aren't religious. We don't do most of the praying bits. Mainly we just focus on the food. That's honey cake at Rosh Hashanah, and potato pancakes at Chanucah. For Passover in April Mum makes something called matzah brie, which is a bit like a cross between pasta and omelette with sugar and cinnamon on top.

Mum asks Alice a few questions. It turns out that Jacob is from London, like us, and he works in theatre.

"He's very creative and interesting, and just so kind and lovely," says Alice. "I do hope you like him."

"Well, that all sounds lovely, darling," says Mum. "I can't wait to meet him."

Alice laughs. "Well, that's good, because I invited him this afternoon."

"You did?" Mum asks.

"You what?" I say.

Mum says it more politely than me, but we're both a bit shocked.

"But it's my birthday," I say, trying not to be rude. Why didn't Alice ask if she could bring a total stranger along to a family event?

"I know," Alice says. "But I'm not in London much, and it's important that you meet him." She stops, then adds, "I shouldn't say anything until he gets here. We want to tell you ... ask you ... together ..."

Mum gets it before me.

"Oh, Alice! Darling!" she says, her eyes filling with tears.

"What?" I demand. "Tell me!"

"Well, Jacob wants to ask Mum – and Dad, of course – if it's OK for us to get married," says Alice.

Just at that moment, the doorbell rings. Alice rushes to open it, leaving Mum and me staring at each other, our mouths open with amazement.

"What?" I say.

"It does seem very sudden," says Mum.

"I think she's gone mad!" I say.

I think it all the more when the door opens and I see Alice standing there with Jacob.

He's short – even shorter than Alice.

His head is totally bald.

He's got a big bushy beard.

And he's really, really, really old. I'd guess forty at least.

Is this a suitable husband for my sister? I think the answer has to be no!

Chapter 4

I can't think of one thing to say to Jacob that isn't, "Who are you, and can you leave my sister alone, please?" So I blush bright red and say, "Actually, maybe I will get changed after all." I almost barge Jacob out of the way to rush upstairs and search my room for something to wear.

There are lots of T-shirts that don't fit any more. Zero nice skirts or dresses. In the end I pull on a white T-shirt that just about fits and some black shorts with a stretchy waist.

But are they a bit short? Well, never mind.

When I go outside, Dad is making very awkward conversation with Jacob, all about his job in theatre. Dad's telling Jacob about the last play he saw, which was *Mary Poppins* about a hundred years ago.

Luckily I don't need to say anything as Adam's arrived. I rush over to say hello.

I really miss Adam, and I'm sad he decided to live in Edinburgh. He's always been a brilliant big brother. He taught me to do cartwheels, and he used to listen to me read when I was in infant school. When I was younger, he used to let me plait his hair. He still explains my Maths homework over Zoom if I get stuck.

"Happy birthday, Miri!" Adam says, and pulls a present out of his bag.

I rip off the paper. What on earth ...?

"Boxing gloves?" I say.

"It's the best exercise!" he raves. "And I thought you might like it as you're not doing your gymnastics any more."

"I didn't have Miri down as a fighter," says Dad.

"Boxing isn't about fighting," says Adam. "It's about fitness. I just thought Miri would enjoy it."

I'm totally taken aback. Why would Adam think I'd like boxing? Does he think I'm kind of butch and mannish and aggressive? What does he see when he looks at me?

"Thank you!" I say, putting on a big smile.

Adam grins back and says, "I promise you'll like it! I'll give you a lesson!"

He insists I put the gloves on and then puts up his hands. "Hit me."

"I can't!" I say.

"Don't worry, you won't hurt me."

"I don't know what to do!"

"Just hit my hand," Adam tells me. "In the centre of my palm."

I tap his hand gently.

"Hit me properly!" he says.

I flail, my arms swinging like windmills.

"Not like that," Adam says, and shows me. "Hit me like this. Look – from the shoulder. Put your weight behind it."

I draw back my arm. I look at Adam's hand and think about throwing all of my body into a punch. And how that would feel. There's something powerful and amazing about that thought, and I let my fist fly forward …

But it misses the target completely and lands somewhere east of Adam's ear. I lose my footing and fly after my fist. He loses his balance, and we both crash to the ground.

Alice and Dad are laughing and exclaiming and pulling us up. We're laughing too, and no one notices anyone else coming into the garden. Until we hear a girl's voice.

"Oh my goodness! Do your family parties always end up in fights?"

I'm suddenly aware of two things. First that my shorts really are very short, making my ginormous, spotty bum all too obvious in this position.

And second, that voice sounds just like Toxic Tiff. It's her sister! It must be!

Oh no!

Chapter 5

Did you ever have a Barbie doll? Because that's what the new arrival reminds me of.

Golden hair.

Blue eyes.

A rosebud mouth, with shiny pink lip gloss outside and dazzling white teeth inside.

A tiny waist, long legs and an impossibly perfect chest.

All wrapped up in a dress the turquoise of a posh hotel swimming pool.

Barbie is pulling Adam up from the ground, with raised eyebrows (straight, black, super sculpted). She lets out a tinkling laugh and says,

"Adam told me he had a lively family! Don't I remember you from school, Miri? You were a very wriggly four year old!"

Adam's laughing too. "We're just trying out Miri's birthday present," he says. "I think she's going to be a great fighter!"

I feel Barbie's eyes scan me. I pull off the boxing gloves and try to adjust my shorts, which seem to have ridden up a bit. That amazing feeling of power and strength I felt when I used the boxing gloves is draining away.

"Happy birthday!" Barbie says, and hands me a present wrapped in candyfloss-pink paper. "This is from me."

"Oh – thanks," I mutter. "You're Tiffany's sister, aren't you?"

I'm still hoping the answer could be no. But she says, "Yes, I'm Scarlett. Tiffany's so excited that I'm going out with her friend's brother!"

Huh! I try hard not to show Scarlett what I think of Tiffany.

"Good coincidence, don't you think?" says Adam, taking her hand. "We couldn't believe it when we got talking in a bar in Edinburgh, totally randomly, and discovered that our sisters were pretty much best friends."

Best friends? Me and Tiff? What?

"You could even say that you and Tiffany brought us together," says Scarlett.

Vomit!

I have to admit, they do look good together. Adam is tall and dark and spends a lot of time at the gym. He has the sort of blue eyes that people call piercing, and his hair flops onto his forehead. Next to him, Scarlett the Barbie girl looks even prettier – even more delicate and feminine and blonde.

They seem much better suited to each other than Alice and short, old, baldy, beardy Jacob. But who am I to judge people's appearances?

"Scarlett and I have got something to tell you all," says Adam. "She's … we've … she's my fiancée."

"Fiancée?" Dad and Mum say it at the same time.

"Surprise!" says Adam. "We thought we'd keep it a secret."

"You certainly did that," says Dad, red in the face. "Does your mother know?"

"We told her last night, before we left Edinburgh," Adam explains. "She was sworn to secrecy. And we told Scarlett's dad in Scotland and her mum here in London this morning." Adam shakes his head and laughs. "I know, I know ... it's been a bit of a whirlwind."

Mum rushes forward to give him a hug – and then Scarlett.

"It's wonderful news!" Mum says. "You'll have to forgive us, Scarlett, if we're a bit surprised."

"Champagne!" says Dad, and disappears into the house.

"This is Alice ..." says Adam. "My step-sister ... and ... err ..."

"This is Jacob," says Alice.

"Oh, hi, Jacob, nice to meet you ..."

"And actually ..." says Alice. She takes Jacob's hand. "We've got some news too."

"Don't tell me – you're getting married too! What are the odds?" says Adam. He's clearly joking, but he didn't hear what Alice just told me and Mum in the kitchen.

Dad emerges from the house with a bottle and a tray of glasses and starts fussing with the cork.

I hold my breath. Surely Alice isn't really going to marry this old guy?

"Yes, we are," says Alice. "This summer. As soon as we can arrange it."

POP! The cork flies out of the champagne bottle and we all gasp and then say things like "Wow!" and "Congratulations!"

All except Scarlett, who looks just a bit annoyed. "Not August 25th, I hope," she says, flashing her sharp white teeth. "Because that's when we're getting married."

"No, we thought end of July," says Alice, lifting her chin.

"That's ... very soon, darling," says Mum.

"Did you know about this?" I hear Dad mutter to Mum.

"They just told me. Jacob asked my permission. It was very sweet ..." Mum whispers back.

Alice waves her hand and says, "It's good timing. We've both managed to get a break. We only want something small anyway."

How can this be happening? Two total strangers joining my family? One of them related to Toxic Tiff, which will make us ... what? Half-sisters-in-law?

"Two weddings!" says Mum, turning to Dad. "We'll be the only unmarried couple in this family, Paul!"

Mum and Dad always say they meant to get married but never got round to it. They were too busy blending their families and having me. And sometimes they say that they each had a big wedding the first time around and didn't really see the point in doing it all again. Whatever.

"Well," says Dad. "What a day!" He lifts up his glass of champagne. "A toast! To Adam and ... umm ... Scarlett, and Alice and ... err ... Jonah ..."

"Jacob!" says Mum sharply.

"Wonderful!" says Dad. "All of you getting married at once ... apart from Miri of course ..."

So then everyone's looking at me, and I want to disappear.

"Happy birthday, darling!" says Mum, and everyone drinks my toast. Then I open the rest of my presents. A manicure set and three pots of glittery nail varnish from Scarlett. A vegan cookbook from Alice and Jacob.

Then they all start talking weddings. Venues! Colour schemes! Dresses! I sit and sip my lemonade, which makes me feel a bit sick. I wonder when we can eat and whether the burgers are going to go off, sitting in the sun waiting to be cooked.

Then I hear Alice say, "And Miri, you're my bridesmaid, OK?"

"And ours!" says Adam.

Scarlett doesn't look all that happy, but she says, "I'm having a bridesmaid squad – five of my closest friends and my three sisters, and I hope you two as well ..."

"I can't possibly as I'm getting married myself," says Alice. "But Miri will represent the family, won't you?"

They're all looking at me. *No, I think. I don't want to be a bridesmaid. No, no, no, no. Not at all. Never. No.*

But I open my mouth and say, "Yes, of course."

Chapter 6

"Lucky, lucky, lucky you," Sophie says to me the next day at school. "You don't know how much I yearn to be a bridesmaid. I dream of it ... I'd literally kill to be a bridesmaid."

"I don't think you literally would," I say. I turn my crisp packet upside down to catch the last crumbs in my palm. It's break time, and I am starving.

"My family is useless," Sophie goes on. "No sisters or cousins! No one that's going to pick me out, dress me in something fabulous and give me a starring role on their big day. Honestly, life is so unfair! You get to be a bridesmaid twice in one summer, Miri – twice. And you don't appreciate it at all!"

"I wish you could do it instead of me," I tell her.

"What's more, you and Tiff get to be bridesmaids together!" Sophie adds. "It would be so perfect if I could ... but never mind."

Sophie looks so disappointed that I tell her I'll try to get her invited to both weddings. "It's better not to be a bridesmaid. You can wear whatever you want, and no one will look at you."

Sophie rolls her eyes. Then she spots Tiffany across the playground. "Tiffany!" Sophie yells. "Get over here! Bridesmaid summit!"

Here she comes, my half-sister-in-law-to-be. Tiff is mincing across the playground, all too aware of the heads that turn to watch her. Loving all the attention. Ugh, I can't stand her.

"Isn't it amazing news?" Sophie greets her. "Did you know Miri's going to be a bridesmaid twice?"

"I heard," says Tiff. "Scarlett wasn't too happy. She thought she'd be the only bride in town."

There's nothing I can say to that.

"There's going to be a whole squad of us bridesmaids," Tiff informs me. "And we're just the junior members. Not even invited to the hen."

"What's a hen?" I say, imagining Scarlett and a massive chicken.

"The hen-do!" Tiff explains. "A whole weekend at a spa hotel in Marbella. Scarlett says she won't take responsibility for teenagers. So Mum says to make up for it she'll take me for a spa day. Maybe you and your mum could come too."

"I'm allergic to spas," I lie.

"Tell me everything," says Sophie. "Where are Adam and Scarlett getting married?"

"Scotland," I say.

"Very romantic," says Tiffany.

"Kilts and bagpipes. Mum says if they insist on serving haggis, she's not coming," I add.

"Scarlett hasn't decided what we're wearing yet," says Tiff. "We've got a shopping trip coming up. Do you want to come, Sophie? I can get you an invitation."

"Oh yes please! And can I come on your other shopping trips, Miri? As your personal style adviser?"

I nod. It's so difficult to say no to Sophie.

"Are you joining our WhatsApp weight-loss group?" asks Tiffany. "I think Scarlett sent an invitation to your mum."

She certainly did. Mum was highly unimpressed. "Does she think I'm fat?" Mum said. "Because if so, Scarlett's starting off on the wrong foot."

"We've got a personal trainer," says Tiffany. "You and your mum could come along to our sessions. I mean, you'd be keeping me company." Tiff laughs.

"That's so nice of you, Tiff," says Sophie, while I fume in silence.

I get out of answering by the bell going. Tiffany and Sophie head for Textiles. I go to Science, where we're mixing chemicals in test tubes. I can pretend I am concocting potions to turn Tiffany into a toad. I imagine walking down the aisle with a tiny green amphibian hopping beside me wearing a tiara, and it makes me laugh.

But then I think of all the people who'll be watching me. I decide I actually want an invisibility potion, and Tiffany can remain human.

At break I get a text from Mum:

We're meeting Scarlett's family tonight. I'll pick you up after school.

Great.

And a text from Alice:

Let's go dress shopping on Sunday?

Superb.

And one from Tiffany:

C U later! We can brainstorm bridesmaid styles!

Oh no!

Chapter 7

Mum says I can't go to meet Scarlett's family wearing school uniform: "Such an unfortunate colour, that green." She suggests that I just slip into a dress that she happens to have picked up in Sainsbury's that afternoon, which she thinks will really suit me.

The dress is in my bedroom, on my bed.

At first I think it's nice. It's burgundy, which I like. It's got a crossover top and a skater skirt and a light brown belt. It looks like it might even fit.

Looks can be deceptive.

The sleeves cut into my arms, the buttons bulge over my chest and the skirt barely skims my knickers.

I'm out of the dress in two minutes. It's back in the bag, with the receipt. And I pull on a baggy black T-shirt and some leggings. My usual.

"Any good?" says Mum hopefully when I come downstairs.

"No," I say. "I didn't like it. I don't like dresses."

"Oh dear," Mum says. "I hope you change your mind before all these weddings. Weddings mean dresses. Heaven knows what I'm going to wear. I wish they'd pick colour schemes at least."

I wonder why weddings have to mean dresses. Wouldn't they be a lot less stressful if everyone could just wear casual clothes?

Scarlett's family lives around the corner, but her house is totally different from ours. We live in an old house in the middle of a terrace, with a small garden at the back and lots of stairs. Our house is full of books and magazines and papers, and Mum is always saying she must tidy up. Our walls are painted in bright colours – red and blue, purple and olive. The floors are stripped wood, and the walls are covered in artworks made by all of us kids over the years. Dad always says that it's amazing how you can make things look good with a frame.

Scarlett's family's house is a modern bungalow, and it is super tidy. There are no books or piles of papers or bits and pieces. All the walls are bright white, and all the carpets are grey and plushy. On the walls there are large framed photographs of Scarlett's mum, Scarlett and her sisters – ugh, Tiffany, grinning down at me. Everyone has the same blonde hair. Everyone has shiny white teeth. Even the cat is a ball of fluffy white fur with bright blue eyes.

Scarlett's mum is super glam, with her blonde hair scraped back into a ponytail. She's wearing a cherry-pink tracksuit, which exactly matches her nail varnish. She shows us into a dazzling green garden, saying, "Astroturf – so much easier than real grass." We sit down on grey rattan sofas. Her eyes scan our bodies up and down. I want to hide, but in this bare garden there's nowhere to run. Scarlett's mum introduces herself: "I'm Joanne. It's so lovely to meet Adam's family."

"Of course, I remember you from Tithe Green Juniors," says Mum. "Miri and Tiffany were in the same class."

Joanne shakes her head. "I can't think of you ... Were you involved with the parents' association?"

Mum now shakes her head and says, "Couldn't stand it – all that competitive volunteering."

"Oh! I was the chair for a while!" Joanne exclaims.

There's a brief silence, which Dad fills by saying, "What a coincidence, eh? Adam and Scarlett meeting up in Scotland but having sisters who went to the same school in London. Who'd have thought it?"

"I gather Adam's real mum is up in Scotland?" says Joanne.

"Yes. I'm just the stepmother," says Mum. "Wicked or otherwise."

Mum's joke falls flat. Joanne just bares her white teeth and says, "Adam's set up a Zoom so I can meet his real mum later on. Obviously we're going to have to co-ordinate colours at the wedding with extreme care."

"Hello, all!" It's Scarlett, carrying a tray of glasses. "Who wants a drink?"

"It's low-calorie, low-alcohol sparkling wine," says Joanne, handing a glass to everyone but me. "I don't know about you, but I want to shift at least half a stone before the big day. And these love birds haven't given us long to get into shape!"

Scarlett rolls her eyes and says, "Sorry, Mum. We just couldn't wait!"

"That's love for you!" Joanne says. "No thought for anyone except yourself! I suppose your dad knew all about it."

"No, really, he didn't," Scarlett reassures her. "I'll go and call the others. You can tell them all about your bootcamp plans."

"Bootcamp?" asks Mum, looking a bit nervous.

"We've got no choice!" Joanne pulls a notebook out of her handbag. "Just under three months to go. I've booked a personal trainer – he'll be here three times a week at 7 a.m. I'm researching beauty therapists." Joanne extends a sharp-nailed finger towards Mum. "That skin tag just under your eye ... I've got a woman in Knightsbridge who can freeze it off for you."

"I … well … thank you," says Mum. Her hand goes to her eye, covering the offending tag – something I'd never really noticed before.

"Scarlett's going plant-based for the duration, but I swear by steak and spinach," Joanne goes on. "And regular massages. And intermittent fasting. I once lost two stone in two weeks! It was a miracle!"

"It doesn't sound very healthy," says Dad.

"Ah, that's a man speaking. We ladies know we're always going to be judged by the size of our hips, aren't we? Oh, here are my girls."

Tiffany has changed out of her school uniform too. She's wearing a cute skater girl dress … which looks very much like the one that Mum bought for me. Same burgundy colour. Same pale belt. She looks great.

"Oh, Miri," says Mum. "Isn't Tiffany's dress the one I picked out for you? From Sainsbury's? See how lovely it looks? You should give it a chance." She shakes her head. "Miri just won't wear dresses right now. Maybe being a bridesmaid will change her mind."

My face is scarlet. I can feel it. I wish Mum would shut up.

"Hey, Miri," says Tiffany. "Did you do that Maths homework yet?"

"Oh, Tiffany!" says her mum. "Literally no one cares about Maths."

Tiffany tosses her curls and says, "Mum, give me a break. Miri, do you want to come upstairs?"

"Stay focused, Tiffany," says Joanne. "We need to get down to business. Colour scheme, Scarlett. Is it going to be purple? Or have you decided on pink? Hurry up! We need to know!"

"Pink," says Scarlett. "And gold. And the bridesmaids wearing different styles, but all in satin."

"Pink!" says Tiffany. "We could all be different sweets – I could be candyfloss, Miri could be bubble-gum ..."

Tiffany would look amazing in candyfloss pink. And bubble-gum pink would match my spots.

"Sweets? I don't think so!" says Scarlett. Tiffany looks a bit disappointed.

"So I gather you've got another family wedding this summer?" says Joanne.

"Yes, my daughter's getting married ..." Mum starts.

"Wonderful!" Joanne shows her teeth in a grin. "So you'll really be the top wedding planner. And will Miri be a bridesmaid for her sister too?"

"She will," says Mum.

"Lucky girl!" Joanne bats her false eyelashes. "I was a bridesmaid when I was about their age, for my sister. What a wonderful experience! I loved getting dressed up, looking after the bride, having my picture taken ..."

"Not everyone is like you, Mum," says Tiffany. I know she means that not everyone is as pretty as her mum – for example, me. I try not to scowl.

"It changed my life," Joanne continues. "All I wanted from that day on was to be a bride. I used to design wedding dresses when I was meant to be doing my homework. I got a job in a wedding-dress shop as soon as I could leave school ..."

I'm waiting for the moment when Joanne tells us that she's a world-famous wedding-dress designer now. Or a wedding planner, or a wedding singer or …

"I got married as soon as I could. I was twenty years old. My waist measured only a few inches more than that!"

"Wow," says Mum. "Well, that's certainly something."

"It didn't last," Joanne adds. "My big mistake. My husband ran off to Scotland with a predatory librarian. She was size fourteen! Can you imagine?"

Scarlett and Tiffany both wince. Clearly being horribly size-ist runs in the family.

"That must have been terrible for you." Mum's voice shakes a bit as if she's trying not to laugh.

"My ex-wife lives in Scotland too," says Dad. "She loves it there. It'll be helpful having them there, on the spot, to do the local planning."

Joanne's mouth is a thin line. "I will not allow that woman—" she begins.

"Danielle," says Scarlett.

"The librarian from hell—"

"Oh, Mum!" Scarlett shouts.

"To take over my big day. I mean Scarlett's big day."

"Adam and Scarlett's big day," says Mum. "And I'd be only too grateful if Adam's mum – Carolyn – and your ex-husband could do some of the planning."

Scarlett waves her phone. "Look! Bridesmaids' dresses!"

"Amazing!" says Tiffany, grabbing it. "Look, Miri, which one do you fancy? Maybe this one?" She thrusts a picture of a girl in a tight pink satin dress at me. The model looks like she's auditioning for a role in a sausage advert.

"Oh!" I say. "Maybe. Hmm. Actually, I haven't done that Maths homework yet. Maybe I should be going home."

"We could do our homework together!" says Tiff.

"My books are at home," I say, lying because all our homework is online.

Mum finishes her drink and says, "It's so lovely to see you again, Joanne. Wonderful to be planning a wedding together. I can't wait to get started."

*

Later, at supper, Mum's oddly quiet.

"Awful woman," says Dad. "Let's hope Scarlett doesn't take after her."

"Hmm," says Mum. "I know what you mean. It feels like she's never got over her divorce. I remember Joanne crying in the school playground one time. But I might pop along to meet her personal trainer. You might want to come too, Miri."

No thanks, I think. But I don't say anything. I'm haunted by the pink-sausage model. Will I look like that?

Please, no.

Chapter 8

The shop is a bit like a scene from *Say Yes to the Dress*. There are rows of wedding dresses, shimmering white and cream, lacy and shiny, sparkly and frilly. There are mirrors, and the changing room with velvet curtains. And here we are, lined up, waiting for Alice to come out of the changing room. Mum. Me. Sophie, who begged to come as unofficial style adviser. And Tiffany, who wasn't invited at all, but once we got here, Sophie got all excited and texted her. Fifteen minutes later she turned up.

"I think Scarlett's planning to go to a more expensive shop," she says in typical Tiffany style, looking around.

"Well, good luck to her," says Mum. "But Scarlett would be crazy not to look here, because this is wedding central."

We're on Fonthill Road, which is a little street at the back of Finsbury Park station that's packed full of wedding-dress shops. Not the posh sort you see on TV, but the sort where people who own wedding-dress shops come to get stock.

"Much more choice," says Mum. "If we can't find something you like in Fonthill Road, Alice, then ... well, we'll need to think more creatively."

But it does mean that there's no sofa for us to sit on while we're waiting for Alice. Mum's found a chair, and the rest of us are sitting on the floor. No champagne from the shop assistants either. But the dresses are just as glam and glitzy as anything I've seen on TV.

Sophie isn't impressed, however. "I'd go for something alternative if I were getting married," she's saying. "Definitely not white. Maybe black. A catsuit maybe. With sequins."

"That's what you think now," says the shop assistant. "But 90 per cent of brides want something more traditional for their big day."

"Is that a real statistic or a made-up one?" says Sophie. "I'm going to google it."

So she does, and she finds a survey which says that 75 per cent of British brides wouldn't want to wear white on their wedding day. Also, nearly half of those surveyed said the dress wouldn't be a secret from their partner. And almost half the brides would make a speech on their wedding day.

"Less than half? Why wouldn't you make a speech?" says Sophie. "Surely a bride would want to talk just as much as her partner?"

"It wasn't common for the bride to make a speech when I got married to Alice's dad," says Mum. "But they couldn't keep me quiet!"

"I'd hate to make a speech," I say. I'm imagining everyone looking at me … judging me. Mixing up my words, getting something wrong. Everyone laughing. My face gets hot, and I feel sick just thinking about it.

Sophie's looking at me. "I don't know why you're so—" she starts, but then the velvet curtains rustle and … here's Alice. Wow!

Her dress is made of white silk, with a bodice that's covered in lace. The long sleeves are sheer lace and the neckline is wide. It's lovely – but there's something old-fashioned about it at the same time.

"Do you think it's showing too much at the top?" says Alice.

"Not at all!" says Mum. "In fact, I was wondering if maybe the sleeves might be a bit shorter ..."

"No, I like the sleeves," Alice says.

"You look gorgeous," I say, because Mum hasn't said it, and Alice does look so beautiful. The white suits her dark hair, and the lace is really pretty.

"It's very flattering," says Tiffany. "Your waist looks tiny with that full skirt."

"Thanks," says Alice. "I'm not sure. There's another one. Hang on ..."

The next dress has a different neckline – much higher. The sleeves are slightly puffed and lacy but not see-through at all.

"It's very Victorian," says Mum. "You look lovely – but it has more of a winter feel to me."

But Alice loves this dress. "This is it," she says, turning round in front of the mirror. "Absolutely perfect."

You'd have thought that was that, but then they get into the details of shoes and veils, head-dresses and tights. Sophie and Tiffany are giggling over something on Tiffany's phone. I let my mind drift away, wondering if I'll ever want to get married myself. It doesn't seem very likely. I can just about imagine meeting someone and maybe wanting to live with them. After all, it's fun to be in a family. But why would anyone want to get all dressed up and have everyone staring at them?

It's not even as if getting married guarantees anything. Look at Tiff's mum and the Predatory Librarian.

Mum got married, and her first husband died. Dad got married, and he and his first wife got divorced. I'm almost glad they never got married to each other so nothing bad could happen. I know that's silly. But if those bad things hadn't happened, I wouldn't even be alive.

"How about you, Miri?"

I come out of my dream to find everyone looking at me.

"It'd be good to sort out one bridesmaid's dress at least," says Mum.

Alice is waving something at me, saying, "Just try this one on."

It's a bluey purple. Or possibly a purpley blue.

It's a soft fabric. "Chiffon – nice," says Sophie.

It's long, with long sleeves and a high Victorian neckline.

It's also huge.

"I'm not sure that's my size," I say. But it's clear to me that everyone thinks I am even bigger and fatter than I really am. Oh my.

"We can take it in," says the shop owner. "We just need to measure you. Give it a try."

"But I really ... don't ..."

No one listens. I'm alone in the changing room with a monster dress. The air smells of dust and sweat. I pull the dress over my head, and it pools round my ankles.

I pick it up and try again. The sleeves flap over my hands. The fabric bunches around my flabby waist.

"Come on out and show us!" says Alice.

I keep my hands crossed in front of my chest to stop the dress falling off.

"It's a bit big ..." I say.

"Oh, but the colour is lovely, Miri!" says Mum. "It just needs altering ..."

I need altering. I wish I could take myself in, make my body fit the shape everyone wants. I wish I could say, "I'm size eight" and have everything fit perfectly.

I wish I could go back in time. I wish I was twelve again and not fourteen.

"Miri, you look lovely," says Alice.

I look in the mirror. I see purple-blue fabric. I see a red-faced girl. I see her messy dark hair. I see sweat shining on her brow and spots bubbling under her skin. If I were a girl in a magazine, I'd be a "before" picture.

I see Tiffany's patronising smirk and Sophie looking unsure.

"It's nice," Sophie says. "But don't you want to be a bit more out there, Alice? A bit more edgy?"

"No," says Alice. "This is perfect. Don't you agree, Miri? We can pick up the blue colour in the flowers and the tablecloths and everything."

What can I say? I'm an accessory, connecting the whole event.

"Oh, yes," I respond. "Yes. Perfect."

Chapter 9

"Wakey, wakey!" It's Mum, it's 6.30 a.m., and she's got an unnatural grin on her face. "Time to get up!" Mum goes on. "We're going over to Joanne's for our personal-training session!"

I pull the pillow over my head. "I am not doing this!"

But Mum's not taking no for an answer.

"Oh yes you are! We have two weddings to get in shape for. And we're meeting Jacob's family soon. And I need your moral support, Miri! You wouldn't make me face those scary girls on my own, would you?"

"This is emotional blackmail!" I say, but I sit up in bed.

"I know!" Mum replies. "But I can't think of another way to get you to come with me ... and I think we should give it a try. Come on. Bridal bootcamp. How bad can it be?"

Very bad is the answer to that. Very bad indeed. Soon we're all lined up in Joanne's front room – me, Joanne, Tiffany, Mum and Tiffany's other sisters, Lola and Lily (who are even more blonde and perfect than Tiffany and Scarlett). And then there's Ronaldo, the personal trainer, who is tanned and dark and "has muscles on his muscles" Mum said to me in a whisper.

Ronaldo gets us stretching. He makes us do sit-ups and push-ups and something called dead bugs. I am sweaty and aching and I hate every minute. And then he opens up a bag of equipment and says, "Gloves for you." He points to Mum, Lily, Lola and me. "And pads for the others. And for me. Then we'll change over."

Not again! Another chance to embarrass myself. Ronaldo puts us in pairs. Mum and Joanne. Himself and Lily, alternating with Lola. And me with a very nervous-looking Tiffany.

"I'm not sure this is a good idea," Tiff says. "Miri's a bit of a monster with boxing gloves on. Scarlett said you knocked out a grown man."

"Nonsense," says Mum. "That was just Adam and Miri messing around."

It's strange – putting the gloves on somehow cheers me up. I remember the feeling of power I had last time. I liked it.

Ronaldo shows us how to stand and some basic moves. "This is a jab. This is the undercut. Excellent for body conditioning. Also stamina."

"We're going to need stamina with two weddings in one summer," says Mum.

We take some practice swipes. I take care to hold back my punches, to tap the pad that Tiffany's holding really gently.

Ronaldo nods at me and says, "Nice movement. Now swing a bit stronger."

It's so long since anyone has given me a compliment like that. Something positive about the way I use my body. It takes me back to those gymnastics classes I used to love. Balancing and tumbling, swinging and moving with grace and ease.

"I loved that dress you chose for your sister's wedding," Tiffany says as I draw back my glove. "Gorgeous colour. Really suits you. It's such a good thing they had a plus-size section."

Somehow I forget to hold back. And when Tiffany sees my fist nearing her at speed, she shrieks ... drops her pad ... and WHAM! I hit her perfect nose, which starts pouring with blood, all over Joanne's carpet.

"Help! No!" screams Joanne, dashing for a box of tissues.

"Miri! Why did you do that?" Mum asks. She clearly thinks I planned to attack Tiffany.

"I didn't mean to!" I say. "She dropped her pad!"

That's the end of the bridal bootcamp. And it's clear that Joanne won't be inviting me back. She's now on the phone to the StainAway Carpet Cleaning Company. Tiff is leaning over the sink, nose plugged with tissues. She offers me a muffled, "Bye, Miri! Don't worry, I'll be OK." I hear the sarcasm dripping from Tiff's voice – a bit like the blood dripping from her nostrils.

But Ronaldo says as he follows us out of the door, "You know, I think you have talent in fighting." He hands me a flyer for a boxing club. "That's the best place. I think you'd enjoy it."

Chapter 10

Mum and Dad really don't like the idea of me going to the boxing club. "Why not go back to gymnastics?" says Mum. "Absolutely no fighting," says Dad. "I don't want you getting injured." But when they look up the club's website, it turns out there is a Boxercise class. So they let me go to that.

"Why not ask Sophie if she wants to go too?" says Mum.

I think that's a good idea. A chance to spend time with Sophie without Tiffany there. And without always talking about fashion. But Sophie's not keen. "I heard what happened to Tiffany's nose," she says. Instead, she and Tiff are having a "very important meeting" about setting up an

Instagram account that they hope will get them lots of free stuff. "We're going to be influencers," says Sophie. "You have to come to the meeting too, Miri. Tiff was saying it wouldn't be the same without you."

My face must show what I think.

"I wish you'd give her a chance!" Sophie says. "Tiff's really nice!"

"I've known her a lot longer than you," I mumble.

"I think you're being too harsh!"

"Never mind," I say. "I'll go to Boxercise by myself."

The gym is big and old and smells of dust and sweat. The room is full of women who look strong and tough and not especially thin or pretty. At first I'm nervous, but then I realise I'm having fun. For a whole hour I forget about Toxic Tiff and the world of Instagram. I don't worry about getting sweaty, because everyone else is too. And I don't even think about weddings.

My favourite bit is when we get to pair up and practise hitting. I get that heady feeling of power again. And all my tension goes into the punches with a *whoosh!* All my anger at Tiffany. All my feelings about how unfair life can be.

At the end the Boxercise teacher asks my name and says, "Have you ever done this before?"

"Not really," I reply.

"Because I think you've got a natural feel for it," the teacher says. "Have a think about coming to some of our other classes. Are you a gymnast? You move like one."

"I was," I say, then hesitate. "I gave up. I stopped when I got Covid, and I don't feel confident any more."

"Well, this can be a good way of getting your confidence back," the teacher says with a smile. "Well done, Miri. Will I see you next week?"

I can't believe that the teacher can see the old gymnast Miri in the new lumbering giant Miri. I can't believe that she thinks I have a natural feel for boxing. I feel myself standing taller, smiling back at her.

"Yes," I say. "I think so. Yes, you will."

Chapter 11

Mum's bought notebooks and a massive wall planner, which she tacks up in the kitchen. She sets up a family WhatsApp called "Weddings Countdown". She shares a million links to wedding-planning websites and people called bridal influencers.

"The key to a successful wedding is treating it like a military operation," Mum says. "Even if not many military operations have to be battled on two fronts."

"Isn't that a bit of an unfortunate metaphor?" says Dad. "After all, we're not actually fighting anyone here. Everyone is very happy."

This is typical Dad. He hates anything to do with fighting. "All I want is a quiet life," he always says. And mostly I agree with him, but sometimes I feel myself really wanting to argue with anyone – about anything. That feeling boils up inside me with nowhere to go. And then I think that maybe I don't want a quiet life at all.

"Hmm," says Mum. "Yes, weddings are happy occasions. But they provide many opportunities for people to fall out. There's even a word in Yiddish for a family row that starts at a wedding. A *broiges*."

Yiddish is a special Jewish language. Mum has been using it a lot more than usual in the run-up to Alice's wedding, mainly because she's been on the phone to her mum a lot. "Jacob's family are nice people but *meshuggenah frummers*," she says. *Meshuggenah* means mad, and *frummer* means religious. That means they are madly religious. And I don't know any madly religious Jewish people. So I'm super nervous about meeting them when we're invited over to their house for tea, followed by something called a *vort*.

"A *vort*!" says Mum. "No one had those in my day apart from the really super Orthodox Jews."

But Alice says a *vort* is something all her friends are doing and it'll be nice, so along we go.

I'm expecting Jacob's family to be like the strictly Orthodox Jews I've seen in north London – the ones with beards and black clothes and hats. But they don't look like that. They just look ordinary and nice and friendly, and no one says anything about bootcamps or getting in shape. Or religion.

Jacob's parents are both doctors – a bit older than Mum and Dad. They make us tea and then we all sit down at a table laden with loads of food – mini bagels with smoked salmon and cream cheese, and five different sorts of cake. They want to talk about who we know that they might know.

Where did Mum grow up? What school did she go to? What about Alice's dad? Was Mum a member of any youth groups? Where did she work? Where did Alice go to school?

I can see Dad looking more and more uneasy and nervous. And Mum's on edge too. At last she comes up with an older cousin that Jacob's mum was at school with – "Rosalie! Such a lovely person!" Everyone looks relieved and happy.

Then Alice and Jacob arrive, off the train from Manchester. I like the way his parents are so nice to Alice and make a big fuss of her. Adam and Scarlett arrive too, holding hands and looking like the perfect couple. I feel a bit sorry for Jacob, because this should be his special day, and yet he just doesn't look like the sort of person that anyone would dream of marrying.

"Miri," Jacob says, "I was wondering ... you might not be interested—"

"I think Miri will be interested," says Alice with a smile that I know is meant to be encouraging.

"I'm running a workshop for young people," Jacob explains. "It's at a theatre in East London that I do a lot of work with, and I just thought maybe you might like to come along. You can bring a friend if you want."

I open my mouth to say no. I hate drama at school. Too many people looking at me. Too many chances to make yourself look silly.

But ... "What a great idea!" says Mum. So of course I have to say yes.

Then more people start arriving. I'm happy to be able to sit quietly in a corner and just watch while Alice is introduced to everyone.

But then I'm grabbed and hugged in a cloud of perfume.

"Grandma!" I say.

"Miri! My darling! It's so wonderful to see you. It's been ages!"

My grandma, Sadie Goldberg O'Reilly, lives in sheltered housing in North London. She tells us that she loves it – she calls it the party house and makes out that it's fun all the time. But she says life is only complete with annual holidays to the Greek sunshine.

Now she's back, tanned and with her hair newly blonde.

"Lovely, lovely Miri," Grandma says. "What on earth has happened to you? So tall! And big! Look at those *pulkes*!"

I'm not sure what *pulkes* are, but she's looking at my thighs, so I don't ask.

"You're really growing up!" Grandma goes on. "What a beauty!"

I discount this. Grandma has no judgement when it comes to her grandchildren.

"And isn't it exciting?" Grandma says. "Alice getting married! And to such a creative person!"

"Oh," I say. "Well, yes." Then I whisper, "What do you think of Jacob?"

She whispers back, "He seems very nice! And I've seen some of the shows he's worked on – he's a genius!"

"He's so old!" I say, and then I feel embarrassed because of course Grandma is even older.

But she laughs and says, "You're only as old as you feel. And you know what they say – better an old nice husband than a young nasty one."

"Is that an old Jewish saying?" I ask. Grandma says no, she just made it up.

Someone is clapping for attention. A rabbi, I think. Once everyone is silent, the rabbi talks about Jacob and Alice and how they share the same goals – helping people, building a home. He talks about how they went together to a cafe where you can decorate china, and they created a plate with drawings and symbols of all their hopes and dreams for the future.

Jacob lifts up the plate. I love it. It has sunshine and a little house and flowers. It has an ambulance and theatre curtains and the sea. It has people all round the rim, all labelled with letters. There's one with an M. Could it be me?

The rabbi takes the plate from them and puts it into a plastic bag. "Can the mothers come up, please?" he asks.

Mum comes forward and so does Jacob's mother. She's carrying something – what is it? Could it be a hammer? What on earth?

"Alice and Jacob have given their word that they will be married," says the rabbi. "And so this is a very happy occasion. It's also a very serious promise. So we will be fulfilling a tradition to underline just how serious it is – and also to remind us that even at times of the greatest joy, there can be sorrow. We're going to ask their mothers to break the plate."

Break the beautiful plate? What?

Mum and Jacob's mum take the plate between them, still wrapped in its bag. And then they count, "One ... two ... three ..." and smash it down hard on the ground. They each take the hammer in turn and give it a bash.

"I've never even seen this done before," says my grandma.

"Is it a new thing?" I ask.

"No, it's an old thing," Grandma says. "But now people like your sister are doing it, so it's new to me."

The banging and smashing is finished, and people are saying "*Mazeltov!*", which I thought meant congratulations. But according to Grandma it actually means, "Good luck – which is what people need when they get married, let's face it. A lot of luck. And a lot of love."

And now everyone is laughing and hugging. Someone hands me a small bag with a piece of china in it.

"Please God by you," the woman says.

Grandma laughs and says, "Not yet! She's only fourteen! Mind you, I met my *beschert* when I was just fifteen. Never looked at another man. I just knew I'd found the right one."

"What's a *beschert*?" I ask.

"It's your other half – the person who completes your soul. My mother said to me,

'Sadie, typical you, finding an Irish Catholic boy that's your *beschert*.' But I knew he was the right one."

Which is all very well, I think, but what if that person dies? Or what if you never find anyone? Are you just half a person? And if you meet someone after your *beschert* dies – like Mum met Dad – how many halves can one soul have?

*

In the car going home, Mum and Dad talk about how nice everyone was and how beautiful Alice looked, how friendly Jacob's family were. They go on and on until I'm dropping off to sleep.

And I think they assume I am asleep.

But I hear Dad say, "Do you think Jacob's family mind that I'm not Jewish?"

Mum replies, "Oh, not that again! Put it out of your mind, Paul! It's really nothing to worry about."

"I can take a back seat if necessary."

"Not at all!" Mum says. "Don't even think about it! You're Alice's dad just as much as you are Miri's dad."

"Yes, but I wouldn't want to embarrass her," Dad says.

"You wouldn't ... of course not ..."

"And what do you think they think about us not being married?"

"Paul, I can't believe you're worrying like this," Mum says. "You know we decided not to get married. It's fine by me! I've had all the fuss of a wedding before."

"But maybe we should have got married. Maybe I've let you down."

Then they start whispering. I really can't hear now, and I fall asleep properly.

*

Later on, when we're back home, I take the shard of china out of the bag. It's got a tiny flower on it, in the same blue as the dress I'm wearing for Alice's wedding.

Maybe it's a sign that it won't be so bad being a bridesmaid after all? A sign that things can be broken but still be valuable and worth keeping?

Or maybe it's just a piece of broken plate?

I just don't know.

Chapter 12

The shop we go to for our dresses for Scarlett and Adam's wedding is very different from the one on Fonthill Road. It's big and grand and there's a row of gold-painted chairs for us to sit on, and a huge gold-framed mirror for us to look at ourselves.

So many bridesmaids! Five of Scarlett's friends, plus Tiffany and her sisters and me.

Then there's Joanne, who wants Scarlett to try on every dress in the shop. She piles them high in the changing room.

"You might as well, darling," Joanne says. "It's a once-in-a-lifetime experience."

"You hope," mutters Tiffany, next to me.

"It's just that I have a pretty good idea of what I want," says Scarlett. "And it's been so difficult to get everyone together on the same day. I think the bridesmaids should try on their dresses first."

"Sweetie, I insist," says Joanne. "I want to video you in all the different styles – I've looked forward to this day for so long. Since you were born!"

Scarlett's forehead creases into a frown. But she goes into the changing room and emerges five minutes later in a mass of tulle. Everyone oohs and aahs, and Joanne films Scarlett doing a twirl. It's going to be a long afternoon.

After five dresses, Tiff whispers in my ear, "This is so messed up. Scarlett's already chosen her dress."

"She ... what?" I say.

"She came here last week, with her friend Amisha." Tiff jerks her head towards a dark-haired, pretty woman who's currently discussing if fitted works better than floaty with Joanne.

"Scarlett's told the shop people to keep quiet about it," Tiff tells me. "Don't say anything, will you?"

I shake my head.

"So why are we doing this?" I whisper back.

"Mum. Of course." Tiff rolls her eyes. "The wedding control freak."

"That's the one!" says Joanne. "Gorgeous, Scarlett! It's the dress of my dreams!"

Scarlett's wearing a dress with a tight fitted bodice, a ring of sequins around her tiny waist and a ballerina-style skirt. She looks stunning. "Wow!" I say, and Joanne beams at me.

"Miri agrees, don't you?" Joanne says. "This is the one. Say yes to the dress!"

"Maybe it's a bit ... sparkly?" says Amisha.

"Oh, do you think so?" says Joanne. She looks so disappointed. "You're so fussy, but I suppose you know best." Joanne turns to me. "Amisha's the editor of *What Wedding Dress?* magazine. She's the expert's expert."

"Yes, I agree, too sparkly," says Scarlett. She sighs. "Let's try another one. Will we ever find the perfect dress?"

Her friends murmur and laugh, and I realise that everyone knows. All her friends. Her sisters. The ladies in the shop. They all know that Scarlett's already said yes to her perfect dress, and this is just a show for Joanne's benefit.

And I can't help feeling a bit sorry for Tiffany's mum. But also sorry for Scarlett and even Tiffany, because it must be difficult living with a mum who dreams about what you'd look like in a wedding dress. I know my mum cares about what I do with my life every single day. Not just one Big Day.

Scarlett comes out of the changing room. There's a hushed silence as she twirls around.

What makes this dress so perfect? Maybe it's the way the ivory silk is cut, or maybe it's the little pearl beads on the bodice. Maybe it's the gently flared skirt, or the way it makes Scarlett's eyes look bluer and her hair shinier.

Or maybe it's just the way Scarlett seems more relaxed and happy in this dress, dancing and twirling in front of us.

"Oh, darling," says Joanne. "It's perfect. This is the dress of my dreams. As long as it's the dress of your dreams. You look absolutely perfect. The most wonderful bride."

"Say yes to the dress!" says Amisha, and we all clap.

Scarlett goes to the changing room to take off the dress and then emerges in jeans and a T-shirt. She's back to being ordinary again. Not exactly Cinderella in her rags, but the magic sparkle is over. Scarlett's just an ordinary person taking a gulp of champagne and stifling a yawn.

"It's exhausting getting married," she says. "I don't think Adam realises what hard work it is."

"And now it's the bridesmaids' turn!" says Joanne. She pulls out a swatch of pink satin. The pink of a strawberry milkshake.

"This is the fabric, and now we need to find your styles."

Oh no!

The next hour is pure torture. I'm forced to try on different dresses – all at least a size too small for me. Lily and Lola debate which style looks "Not too bad" on me. I watch Tiffany look amazing in every single dress while I feel anxious and out of place and all wrong.

But in the end it's done. And as we walk out of the shop, Amisha catches my eye. "Don't worry," she says. "You're not feeling it now. But wait until you're in your dress, and your hair and make-up are done. Then you'll feel like a princess. I've seen it a million times."

"Really?" I say.

"One hundred per cent yes!" Amisha says. "There's a magic about the big day. I've told Scarlett – it all comes together, all the doubts and worries disappear …"

"Come on, Amisha," calls Scarlett. "We're going for a coffee."

I watch as they walk away, poised and perfect.

Scarlett having doubts and worries?

No way.

Chapter 13

Sophie wants to come to Jacob's theatre workshop – of course, she loves drama. She makes me ask if Tiffany can come too. "You're way too hard on her," Sophie says.

"Me? Hard on Tiffany?" I can't believe my ears.

"It'll be more fun if she comes," says Sophie.

And I feel sad because I'm clearly not entertaining enough myself. "OK," I say.

"Tiff's worried about the wedding," says Sophie. "Her dad is going to be there, and her stepmother, and she thinks it'll be awkward with her mum."

I try to imagine someone who looks like Tiff having actual worries – when she's so blonde, so thin, so gorgeous. I can't do it. Surely everything is pretty much perfect if you look like her?

Mum's glad we've got something to do that day, because she's going shopping with Alice to buy three dresses for herself.

"Three mother-of-the-bride outfits!" Mum says. "It's a nightmare!"

"But there are only two weddings. And you're not mother-of-the-bride at Adam's wedding," I point out. "What's the third dress for?"

It turns out that the week before Alice and Jacob's wedding, there's something called an *aufruf*, when we all have to go to synagogue.

"It's not a huge deal," says Alice.

"It's a huge enough deal that I need a new dress," says Mum. "And the dress for Scarlett and Adam's wedding has to be a particular shade of pink. After hours of discussion with Joanne and Carolyn, I've ended up with raspberry."

We never really talk much about Dad's first wife, Carolyn. In fact, I've only met her once – at Adam's university graduation. Carolyn seemed really friendly then and joined in with the big family lunch we had afterwards at a restaurant. Dad's completely calm about seeing her, but Mum is totally stressing out about things like wedding photos and table plans.

"I'll just fade into the background," Mum tells me. "But I want to look great while fading, if you see what I mean."

I don't really, but I'm just glad I don't have to go on that particular shopping trip.

*

The day of the theatre workshop arrives, and Sophie's got a cold. Her mum won't let her go. So it's just me and Tiffany getting the train to East London together. On the way she asks me all about Alice and Jacob's wedding. "What's Jacob like?" Tiff says. "How long have they been seeing each other? What does he actually do?"

It's exhausting and a bit embarrassing because it makes me realise how I hardly know anything about him. In the end I claim to have a headache and put in my headphones to shut Tiff up. By the time we arrive at the theatre she's got the message and stopped talking.

I'm nervous about the workshop, but I can't help feeling excited as we walk into the theatre. The workshop starts with a tour of the theatre itself, which is all gold and red, with velvet seats and curtains. Then it's into a big airy room with about twenty other kids our age, and Jacob.

I've got an idea of Jacob in my head as someone who's quiet and shy. But this Jacob is different. He gets our attention and makes us laugh. He tells us that the aim is to have fun, that there's no right or wrong, that no one will be giving us marks or reports. And then Jacob says, "Let's start with the yes game."

"I don't know this one," I whisper to Tiffany.

"Don't worry," she says. "I don't either."

For just a moment I forget how annoying she is.

The yes game is easy, explains Jacob. You have to have a conversation and every reply has to start with yes. The more ridiculous the better. The conversation goes on until someone forgets to say yes.

I know that I'm going to be terrible at this before we start.

The first pair to try it have a conversation about an elephant walking down the high street. "Did you see that elephant?"

"Yes! Shall we take it home?"

"Yes! Do you think it likes drinking beer?"

"Yes! But will the elephant fit in our flat?"

"Yes! And shall we get it to ballet dance?"

"Yes!"

The next pair have a conversation about robbing a bank. And then it's Tiffany and me.

"You go first," says Jacob, nodding at Tiffany.

She gulps a bit. "My mind's a total blank!" Tiff says.

"Yes, I can't think of anything either," I say.

"Yes, I find this kind of thing really hard," she gulps.

"Yes, it's kind of difficult," I reply.

"Yes, especially when ..." Tiffany swallows. "I don't think you actually like me, do you?"

What the actual???

"Yes, of course I do!" I say, hoping I sound convincing.

"Yes?" says Tiff.

"Umm, yes!"

"Yes, that's great news!" Tiffany beams.

"Yes, you are being ridiculous!" I can't help laughing. This is such a silly conversation to be having in public, yet somehow the fact that we're playing a game lets me say it.

"Yes, because we've got loads in common," Tiff shoots back.

"Yes, like we both have the same best friend. Who was my friend first," I say.

"Yes, I know," Tiff replies. "I'm grateful to share her with you."

"Yes, that's actually really nice of you to say that."

"Yes, so can we be properly friends now?" Tiffany's voice is hopeful. I have to remind myself that she is acting.

"Oh, of course," I reply.

Jacob claps his hands. "That's it!" he says. "You forgot a yes. Interesting stuff. I think a lot of people could relate to those characters."

What characters?

After we've all had a go, Jacob explains that the yes game is meant to put us in a positive frame of mind. And it seems to have worked, because I stop feeling self-conscious and start having fun. I don't mind at all when Jacob asks us to improvise a play that uses all the best lines of the conversations we've just had.

And I wonder if I should start doing this in life. Perhaps I need some practice at saying yes?

Chapter 14

After the workshop, we have lunch with Jacob at a vegan cafe round the corner. He's funny and interesting as he tells us about some of the shows he's worked on. I stop thinking about how Jacob is old and short and not very exciting looking. Instead I notice how his eyes are brown and twinkly and his smile is warm and genuine. I realise he is just as interested in Tiffany and me as he is in talking about himself.

"Are you excited about being bridesmaids?" Jacob asks.

"Oh yes," I say, as if I'm still playing the yes game.

But Tiffany sighs and says, "I'll be glad when it's over, no lie."

"Really?" I say. I'm amazed.

Tiff takes a bite of her vegan chocolate cake.

"Wedding, wedding, wedding all day every day," she says. "Mum's obsessed. And everyone is so tense. Scarlett's crying all the time. It's a nightmare."

"Oh, Tiffany," I say. "I had no idea. I'm really sorry."

"I hope our wedding isn't causing any tension," says Jacob, looking worried.

I'm not sure how honest to be.

"I think my dad's feeling a tiny bit worried," I say. "Because he's not Jewish at all, and the wedding is going to be very, very Jewish."

"Oh no!" says Jacob. "Alice assured me your dad was OK with it all!"

"The thing about our family is that we never actually say what we think," I tell him. "Because we don't like to cause trouble."

"That's just like our family!" says Tiffany. "Apart from Mum, who always says exactly what she thinks and never understands that she might upset people."

"And what would you say," says Jacob, "if you could say anything you wanted?"

"I'd tell my mum to stop going on and on about how people look," says Tiffany. "And I'd tell her that my favourite subject at school is actually Maths."

"Maths?" I say. I'm thunderstruck.

"And what about you, Miri?" asks Jacob.

"I'd say that ..." I swallow. "I'm not really very sure I want to be a bridesmaid."

"Right," Jacob says. "I understand. I know Alice has set her heart on you playing a really important role at the wedding. But let's see what we can do to make it something positive for you. Do you trust me?"

"Yes," I say. "Yes, I do."

After lunch, Tiffany asks if we can see the theatre's wardrobe department. "So we can tell Sophie about it," Tiff explains. "She's obsessed with clothes."

"Of course," says Jacob. "Who is Sophie?"

"She's my best friend," Tiffany and I both say at once.

"Sounds like a very special person," Jacob says.

"She is! She's very funny and nice," I say.

"And creative and stylish," says Tiffany.

"Do you think it'd be more fun to be a bridesmaid if Sophie was there?" Jacob asks.

"Definitely!" Again Tiff and I both say the same thing at once. And then laugh.

Then we go back into the theatre. Jacob introduces us to Julie, an older lady with grey hair, dressed in a bright pink sari.

"Welcome to the best bit of the whole theatre," Julie says. "This is where the magic happens."

She can see that I'm not convinced.

"Clothes – or costumes – can make you into anyone you want to be," Julie goes on. "The right dress can transform you into a fairy princess, or a crocodile, or whatever you want to be."

"Miri," says Jacob, "if you could have any dress you wanted, what would it look like?"

I shrug and say, "I have no idea."

"It'd be black," says Tiffany. "Miri likes black. And it needs to be the right shape so she can be a kickass fighter in it."

"Oh, of course," says Jacob. And I have to admit to myself that Tiffany knows me better than I realised.

Then we go and look at the racks of clothes in the store. Princesses and witches, woolly jumpers and baggy tweed jackets. Huge satin ballgowns, circus clowns and beggars' rags. Tiffany is touching everything and taking pictures on her phone and asking if she can try things on. And even I try on some big hats with feathers, and a furry wrap.

At the end Jacob says he's had an idea and asks if I mind if Julie measures me up. I do mind, but she does it quickly and she doesn't say anything about my measurements. She just writes them down. And then she measures Tiffany too.

"Tell us why?" says Tiffany, but Jacob says it's a secret.

"Trust me," he says. "I think you'll like it. But will you try to forget about it?"

"Yes!" we say.

Chapter 15

The weddings have taken over our lives. And not in a good way.

Mum is always weighing and measuring herself, worried about whether she'll fit into the dresses she's bought. She goes off to Joanne's bootcamp and comes back grumpy and depressed. Then she's faced with a breakfast of just black coffee and a hard-boiled egg.

Dad tries to cheer Mum up, but she snaps his head off. "It's all right for you! You just need a suit and no one will look at you."

"Actually, Adam wants me to wear a kilt."

"Oh, well, no one's going to be looking at your bottom," says Mum, "calculating how many croissants you eat for breakfast!"

"I think you're letting Joanne get to you, sweetheart," Dad says. "No one's going to be doing that—"

"I need to look good at these weddings! Stop patronising me!"

"Do me a favour and eat something other than a boiled egg," Dad urges Mum. "Anything that's going to put you in a better mood! Have a biscuit! You're beautiful just as you are!"

"Oh, do shut up!" Mum replies. "Alice and Jacob are coming for supper, so I'm saving up my calories for that! Put those biscuits away!"

My parents never fight like this. It makes me wish no one had invented weddings.

Mum makes salmon for dinner, with rice and roasted vegetables. Jacob praises every little thing about it. Alice just pushes the food around on her plate.

"Eat up, Alice!" says Dad. "Don't tell me you're on a silly diet too, like your mother. Tell her she doesn't need to lose any weight. Neither of you do!"

I pile rice and salmon onto my fork and take a big mouthful. But suddenly it doesn't taste so good. I feel invisible, wondering why Dad didn't mention me. And at the same time all too visible – because Dad thinks I definitely should be on a diet, duh. And I can see from Mum that it's no fun at all, punishing herself, but I can also see the way that weddings put you on display.

But then we're always on display. According to Grandma and Mum, back in the olden days you'd only have your photograph taken on special occasions like weddings or holidays. Now it's all day, every day.

"I'm sorry," says Alice. "I'm not actually dieting. In fact, I mustn't lose any weight because the dress won't fit properly if I do. It's just that I'm nervous – there's so much to organise ..."

"It's all in hand," says Jacob. "Don't worry so much."

"It's just ... the *chuppah*, and the rabbi ... and the whole thing really ..." Alice says.

"What do you mean?" Jacob asks.

I feel sorry for Jacob. He looks worried under his beard.

"I not sure the rabbi really understands just how ... complex my family is!" Alice says.

"Of course he does," Jacob replies. "It's really not so unusual. Lots of people have non-Jewish partners. It's not so strange."

I can tell that Jacob is trying to be reassuring, but Mum and Alice both wince, and Dad looks hurt that he's been singled out. Jacob apologises, and everyone tells him that it's fine, they understood what he meant. But that only seems to make us all feel even more awkward.

Just then there's a knock at the door. I run to answer it. Adam's standing there, out in the pouring rain, with no umbrella, getting soaking wet. And he looks as upset as I've ever seen him.

"Adam!" I say. "Why are you here? What's happened?"

"It's Scarlett!" Adam comes in, rain trickling down his face. He shakes himself like a Labrador. I hand him a towel from the downstairs loo. He just stands there, holding it.

"We had a huge row," Adam says. "It was about nothing really – first the wedding list, then the table plan ..."

"Well, that doesn't sound—" I start to say.

"It escalated. It turned into 'You don't listen to me' and 'I'm not sure I'm doing the right thing' ..."

"Oh, Adam!" I say.

Jacob and Alice come out of the kitchen. They hardly seem to notice that we're here, because they're arguing in angry whispers.

"But you know I didn't mean to insult your family!" Jacob says.

"I do know!" Alice replies. "But I think you should just go now! Before you make things worse!"

Jacob blinks hard. "OK. If you think so. But I need to thank your parents—"

"It's OK! I'll tell them you were called away!"

Jacob's very pale. He steps back and nods at Adam and me. "Good night. I'll – I'll call you tomorrow, darling Alice."

"OK," she says, and shuts the door behind him. Then Alice bursts into tears.

I hurry to give her a hug. Adam just stands there looking hopeless.

"I don't know," says Alice. "Maybe I'm making a terrible mistake."

"That's exactly what Scarlett said to me! And now she's not even returning my calls!" Adam buries his face in the towel.

Oh no!

But then I think that if both weddings get cancelled, I won't have to be a bridesmaid at all.

Yes!

Chapter 16

I get my miserable siblings to come back into the kitchen, where Mum and Dad are bickering over the washing-up. I log on to Deliveroo and order churros (Adam's favourite dessert – it's a sort of long crispy doughnut) and chocolate mousse (always goes down well with Alice). Then I make everyone tea and ask what happened.

Out it all comes. Jacob ... Scarlett ... unreasonable ... demanding ... impossible. Annoying ... snappy ... bossy. Disagreements about wedding lists ... table plans ... flowers. Misery! Despair! Stress!

The food arrives, and I hand out the goodies. Everyone seems pleased. No one fusses about wedding diets. Mum says, "You know, sometimes comfort food is just what you need."

"You're telling me," says Adam, chomping on a churro. "Scarlett's been policing my meals for weeks. And her mum's been policing hers."

"Honestly, that woman," says Mum, sneaking a spoonful of Alice's mousse. "Joanne sucks all the joy out of wedding preparation."

"What joy?" says Alice. "It's all just stress."

I nod. I'd be the first to agree about weddings being stressful. But then I shift in my seat and – ouch – something jabs my thigh. I put my hand in my pocket. It's the shard of china from the plate that was smashed at Alice and Jacob's engagement party.

"What about your plate painting?" I ask through a mouthful of churros. "Wasn't that fun?"

Alice brightens. "Oh yes, that was lovely. We talked about the home we want to make ..." She gulps. "Full of people and love – just like here, Mum ... and Dad ..."

"Oh, Alice, darling," says Mum.

"And full of tradition and music and books ..." Alice adds.

"And flowers," says Mum. "I saw beautiful blue flowers on that plate."

"Jacob painted them!" Alice's dark eyes fill up with tears. "He's really romantic. And creative! But sometimes he can be a bit tactless ..."

"Oh well," says Dad. "So can everyone. The times I've tried to cheer up Miri and ended up with my foot in my mouth!"

"That's true." Alice beams at Dad. "Actually, Jacob makes terrible jokes – just like you ..."

"Why don't you ring him?" I suggest. My chances of dodging my bridesmaid duties seem to be fading away. "Jacob was brilliant at the theatre workshop," I add.

Then the doorbell rings. Could Deliveroo have accidentally sent more churros?

But no, it's Jacob, looking nervous and strained and carrying a massive bunch of flowers. "Is Alice ... Do you think she'll see me? I said something all wrong ... I'm not even sure what ... I didn't want to leave it overnight ..."

I usher Jacob into the living room. "Don't worry!" I whisper. "I think it's going to be OK."

"Oh, thank you, Miri. I can't tell you ..." Jacob blinks. "I really do love her with all my heart ..."

"I know!" I say. "And she does too!"

"I know everyone thinks I'm too old for her ..."

"I don't – not at all," I say.

"I'm thirty-five—"

"Oh, that's loads younger than I thought!"

I slap my hand over my mouth, but luckily Jacob laughs and says, "I went bald at twenty-five – what can I say?"

I tell him that Alice's nickname was always "the old lady", and then I think I'd better go and get her.

And when I do, Alice looks so happy that I don't really worry too much about them any more.

I realise that loads of people feel self-conscious about how they look. Even men. Even brilliant theatre directors of thirty-five.

And what matters is if someone is kind and nice and honest and loving. And willing to apologise if they get it wrong.

OK, so I'll have to wear a stupid long dress and have my picture taken. But is it worth it, to be bridesmaid to two people who seem to love each other very much?

Yes, I think it is.

Anyway, it's only one wedding. Happily, the one with the terrible pink dress still seems to be off.

Then my phone vibrates. A text from Tiffany:

TOTAL MELTDOWN HERE! MUM IS SCREAMING AT SCARLETT! SHE IS IN FLOODS! CAN YOU HELP???

What can I say?

I text back: **Yes?**

Chapter 17

Adam's still in the kitchen with Mum and Dad, staring bleakly at a phone that never rings.

I think about a life related to Toxic Tiff. But actually she's not so toxic after all.

I think about the pink satin bridesmaid dress and how it strains over my bum. But a dress is just for a day. A marriage could be for life.

Would it be really selfish of me if I just ... left Adam to it? If I didn't try to make things better?

But it's horrible to see my brother so miserable. "I really thought she was The One," Adam's telling Mum.

There are some problems that can't be solved with churros and chocolate mousse.

"I'm just popping out," I say to Mum. "Sophie needs some help with her homework."

"I don't want you walking over there in the dark!" Mum says.

"Don't worry," I say. "I'll ask Jacob and Alice to take me."

Sometimes it's very useful having older half-siblings and even half-siblings-in-law. Jacob's only too happy to give me a lift to Tiffany's.

I text Tiff from outside: **I'm here, let me in?**

I'm kind of shocked when I see her. Her blonde hair is flat and greasy. She's got a spot on her nose. She's wearing jogging bottoms and a T-shirt, and her eyes are puffy. She doesn't look perfect. She looks just ... ordinary.

"I'm so glad you're here!" Tiffany whispers. "Mum's angry with Scarlett, and Scarlett's really upset. I think the wedding is off!"

"Adam's so unhappy," I whisper back. "But I don't know what it's all about."

"Scarlett says she feels they've rushed into getting married," says Tiffany. "And Mum is being Mother-of-the-bride-zilla."

"Where does that name even come from?" I wonder. "Bride-zilla? I mean, I know it means a bride who goes over the top ..."

"It's from Godzilla," says Tiff. She pulls out her phone and shows me a picture of Godzilla, the giant sea monster, battling with King Kong.

"But that doesn't look like your mum at all," I say, and before I know it I'm giggling with Toxic Tiffany. We're both trying to hold in the laughter with hands over our mouths.

I remember Sophie saying "You're way too hard on her," and I feel bad. Maybe sometimes I just thought Tiffany was being toxic because I was feeling a bit prickly. Maybe I was a little bit toxic myself. I was Kong to her Godzilla.

"What are we going to do?" I ask Tiff.

"Can you say you've come with a special message from Adam?"

"But ... I haven't. He doesn't know I'm here."

"Maybe we should sort of make something up on his behalf?" Tiff says.

"Can we? Should we?"

"We probably shouldn't," Tiff says. "But you could call him?"

I agree. So we go up to Tiffany's room and FaceTime Adam.

"Adam? It's me, Miri. I just thought … I could give Scarlett a message. If you want."

Adam sounds a bit confused.

"What do you mean?" he asks.

"You said she wasn't taking your calls," I say. "But I could tell her …"

"But … I don't know what to say. I don't know what I've done wrong …"

"She's finding all the wedding stuff too much," says Tiff. "Tell Scarlett you don't care about any of it."

"I don't care about any of it!" Adam says.

"And tell her you really love her," I add.

"Of course I do!"

"OK, say all that and send it to me as a video," I say. I add, "Not that I'm telling you what to do, but I am your bridesmaid, so I feel kind of responsible for your happiness."

And then Tiffany sticks her head in and says, "I'm your bridesmaid too, and I know Scarlett's really sad about having argued with you."

Then we wait … and wait … We try not to wince too much when we hear screams and wails and "How could you do this to me?" from Tiff's mum downstairs.

Tiffany sighs. "The thing about my mum is that she never really moved on from splitting up with my dad. I think it's because her whole life peaked on her wedding day."

"That's … really sad," I say.

"I know. Don't tell her, but I'm never going to get married."

"Never?" I say.

"Absolutely never," Tiff replies. "I'm going to be a pilot and travel the world."

"Are you? Wow." This is a whole new side of Not-So-Toxic Tiff.

She's blushing. "Don't tell Mum!"

"I won't," I promise.

Then my phone pings, and Adam has sent a video. We're both desperate to watch it.

"Should we? Just to check it's OK?" asks Tiff, but I shake my head.

"Nope," I say. "It's not for us."

"You're right."

We go downstairs, and Tiffany hands my phone to Scarlett. "You need to watch this – in private," Tiff says.

"What is it?" says her mum. But Scarlett's already halfway upstairs.

I really should go home, but I can't until Scarlett gives me my phone back. So I sit stiffly on the sofa while Joanne quizzes me about what Scarlett is watching, and do I think Adam will ever forgive her, and is all hope lost?

All I can do is shrug and say sorry – I don't know.

At last Scarlett comes down the stairs. She's pale, and her eyes are red, but she's not crying any more. She hands me back my phone.

"Well?" demands her mother. "What's happening? Is the wedding back on?"

Scarlett blinks away her tears. "Yes!"

Chapter 18

It's Alice and Jacob's wedding day. We're in a posh hotel, and the air smells of hairspray and flowers and Grandma Sadie's strongest perfume.

I'm looking at myself in a long mirror. The purple-blue dress has been taken in, and it fits. I have make-up on, which covers the massive spot that erupted on my chin two days ago. ("It's from stress," said Mum.) My hair has been washed and blow-dried, and I have a hairclip at the back of my head. It looks pretty, with silvery petals and leaves, but feels as if some gigantic insect is sitting there. And I am wearing silver ballet pumps which, again, look pretty but are fairly slippery. I'm terrified of falling over.

It's burning hot outside, so in the hotel room the air conditioning is blasting out at super strength, and it's as icy as the Arctic. Yet I can feel sweat trickling down the back of my neck. It must be nerves.

Luckily no one is looking at me, because everyone is just dazzled by Alice. She looks like an old-fashioned princess. Mum is adjusting the veil on the back of Alice's head.

"Oh, darling," says Mum, giving Alice a very careful hug. "Your dad would be so proud. I wish he could see you."

My stomach squeezes tight. If Alice's father were here, that would mean Mum had never met my dad, which would mean ... I'd never have been born. So it sort of feels as if Mum's saying she wishes that she'd never met Dad and that I'd never been born, even if it's just for this wedding. I know she isn't saying that – but that's how it feels.

Alice takes a deep breath. "I do miss him," she says. "But luckily you met just the right person to be my new dad. And I got a brilliant new sister, and a stepbrother as well. And I do think my dad is here today – sort of. I can feel his love anyway."

And then we're all blinking away the tears, while Mum says, "Think of your mascara, girls. No tears now!"

There's a knock at the door – it's Jacob's mum. "Are you ready?" she says. "Time to come downstairs!"

She leads us down to a room where everything is black and white and gold – a chequered floor, golden chairs, a black sofa. "It's like a film set!" says Grandma Sadie, while Jacob's mum makes Alice sit on the sofa.

"Right in the middle, there," she says to Alice. "And your sister next to you."

There's a photographer taking pictures, and Jacob's sisters and aunts and cousins are milling around. Some of Alice's friends are here too. And everyone is so nice that I almost forget I'm wearing a long dress and silver slippers, with a massive ... thing ... on the back of my head.

And then there's mumbling in the room. "Here he comes!" says someone.

The door opens. It's Dad and Jacob's dad, and Jacob and a bunch of his friends.

I'm amazed, because the one thing I know about weddings is that the bride and groom don't see each other until the actual wedding ceremony. (I mainly know that from watching *Married at First Sight*, which if you ask me is a terrible advert for the whole idea of getting married.) But this seems to be a way in which Jewish weddings are a bit different from anything I've seen on TV.

They lead Jacob to the sofa. The look on his face when he sees Alice is like nothing I've ever seen before. Every single bit of Jacob's face looks happy, and his eyes are almost closed because he's smiling so hard.

"Is this the right one?" a man asks him, and everyone laughs.

Jacob nods and says, "Oh yes, it is," and Alice grins up at him.

Then Jacob takes Alice's veil in his hands and pulls it forward so it covers her face. Everyone oohs and aahs, and they take another million photographs. Being a bride – or even a bridesmaid – is a bit like being a celebrity.

"What was all that about?" I hear Scarlett say. Mum explains that it's called a *Bedecken* and it's from the bit in the Bible where Jacob (not our

Jacob, the Bible one) is tricked into marrying the wrong sister by his wicked father-in-law. And I wonder how the wrong sister felt about that, not to mention Jacob, and the other sister, who only got married to him a full seven years later. While Jacob was still married to her sister. Not a great family set-up all round. And an even more complicated one than mine.

And then it's time for the actual wedding, and everyone goes off to find their seats. Everyone apart from Alice and me and Mum and Dad. I've been assuming that I walk behind Alice, but it turns out that's not the case. I have to walk all by myself. Before anyone else.

Suddenly I feel completely sick. Sweat prickles under my arms. My energy drains away. *Everyone's going to be looking at me!* I think I am going to throw up.

Luckily Mum notices that I'm looking terrified.

"I don't think I can do it," I whisper. "There are so many people."

"It'll take two minutes, if that," Mum says.

"I know …" I say. My stomach tilts. "I might throw up."

"Tell you what," says Dad. "I'll walk with Miri. And then you two can walk on your own."

"Really?" I say, relieved. But then I see how disappointed Alice looks. "No," I say. "I can do it."

The ceremony is being held in a garden outside the hotel. There's a canopy, also called a *chuppah*, which has been decorated with pink and purple flowers. Jacob is already standing under the canopy with his best man, his parents, Alice's grandparents, Grandma Sadie and two other men who I guess are rabbis. Luckily it's a pretty big space. On each side there are rows of chairs – women sitting on one side, men on the other. All I have to do is walk from the hotel door to the canopy. Alice and Mum and Dad will follow.

That's all. It doesn't sound much. But there's a photographer and a man with a video camera, and at least a hundred people watching. The sun is beating down, my dress is making me far too hot, and … and … I really don't think I can do this.

I gulp a few times, wipe the sweat from my brow and wish that something could happen to save me. Like the canopy could be struck by lightning. Or Alice could suddenly announce that she doesn't want to get married at all. But that would be awful.

I've never seen Alice look so happy. Jacob looks happy too. And Mum and Dad. There must be something special about weddings.

Sometimes you have to do something for someone else no matter how uncomfortable it makes you feel. Sometimes you have to forget your own fears out of love for someone else. I can do this.

Now. This is it. Time to put on my bridesmaid smile.

It's OK at first. I fix my eyes on the back of Jacob's head and take one step and then another. *No one is looking at you*, I lie to myself. *No one cares. You're not going to make a fool of yourself. You're not going to fail.*

I still feel nervous and shaky. And then my ballet slipper gets caught in the hem of my dress, so I lose my footing and stumble …

I wobble but manage to regain my balance. I make it all the way to the front, where Jacob grins at me. "Well done," he whispers.

Then everyone falls silent, and someone starts to sing – a haunting, lovely tune that reminds me of every time I've been to a synagogue with Mum.

Everyone turns to see Alice walking towards us, with Mum on her right and Dad on her left. They are all so smiley and happy that I forget everyone is looking at me. At us. At Alice and Jacob mostly.

I take Alice's flowers from her and then watch as she walks slowly and carefully around Jacob seven times. She doesn't even stumble once. And then there's the ceremony, which includes both Alice and Jacob sipping wine from glasses held by their mums. If I had to do that, I'd probably dribble the wine down my chin or drop it on my dress. But they manage just fine.

The rabbi gives a speech all about how they will create a new home and invite in guests, and how a wedding is just the beginning of their new life and a new family. He talks about how hard it was that Alice lost her father so young. But then the rabbi says it was wonderful that Mum found a new partner, and how much Alice loves her stepfather. And from the smile on my dad's face, I know he's not feeling awkward and out of place any more.

Then it's time for Jacob to stamp on a glass, which has been wrapped up so no one will get hurt by flying shards.

"We do this to remember the destruction of the temple," says the rabbi. "And to remind ourselves that on our happiest occasions there is still always sadness." And I see Alice's other grandma – the mother of her dad – wiping away a tear.

Then Jacob brings down his foot with a *bang!* Everyone shouts, "*Mazeltov!*" and claps, clarinet music blares out, and their friends form circles and start to dance.

I don't move. No way am I going to risk falling over.

But then Adam says, "Hold on tight." He and some of Jacob's friends lift me up on a chair and dance around with me at shoulder height. I'm shrieking and begging them to put me down.

But the music is infectious, and everyone is laughing and happy. It's fun to feel part of it. And I think that I approve – if this is what weddings are like, I like it. It's actually fun.

And when they put me down, I'm laughing and dancing with everyone else.

"Are you having a good time, Miri?" says Mum.

I'm amazed that the answer is yes.

Chapter 19

The real surprise comes after the wedding ceremony. We pose for hundreds of photos, and then Jacob's mum comes up to me.

"Miri?" she says. "We've got a surprise for you!"

Jacob's mum leads me upstairs to the room where we got changed. But now there are two more people in there – Tiffany and Sophie. "Oh wow!" I say.

"Jacob invited your friends," says his mum. "He thought it'd be more fun for you."

"We kept it a total secret!" says Sophie.

"We saw the whole ceremony," says Tiffany. "It was fabulous. So much more interesting than normal weddings. Maybe I'll get married after all if I can have something exciting like a Jewish wedding!"

"You walked perfectly," says Sophie. "We could tell you were worried."

"Your face!" says Tiffany.

"But only because we know you really well," adds Sophie.

"You were superb at taking the flowers from Alice – not the easiest job," adds Tiff.

"And here," Jacob's mum says as she opens the wardrobe. "Julie from the theatre has made dresses for all of you."

"Oh!" I whisper.

The dresses that she pulls out don't look anything like my purple-blue bridesmaid's dress. Sophie's is ruby red, Tiffany's is sapphire blue and mine is shimmering dark green trimmed with peacock feathers.

"It's ... it's beautiful!" I say.

"Try it on!" Jacob's mum says.

I'm worried until the dress is over my head and zipped up. It's long and soft and it fits. Really fits – every little bit. There's nothing that feels too tight or too baggy.

I look in the mirror and I see ... I see me. I look happy. I look powerful. I look confident and even ... perhaps ... cool.

"Wow!" says Sophie.

"Perfect!" says Tiffany.

I do a twirl in front of the mirror.

"Do you like it?" asks Jacob's mum.

"Yes!" I say. "I do!"

Chapter 20

A month later it's the morning of Adam and Scarlett's wedding ...

The pink dress is even worse in reality than I thought it would be.

The fabric is shiny and bright, and the fit is tight. I have to breathe in to get the zip up. When I breathe out, the dress grips me in a death-squeeze hug. And the shoes – silver sandals – are too high and also too tight.

"You look great!" says Tiffany. "The colour really suits you."

I've realised that when I thought Tiff was being sarcastic, she actually wasn't. I'd added that filter in my head. She doesn't always tell the honest truth – who does? – but she's trying to be nice. Sophie was actually correct.

"I'm not feeling it," I say. "But so what? No one's going to be looking at anyone apart from Scarlett. And she looks amazing."

We're in a hotel room in Edinburgh, and Scarlett hasn't even got into her dress yet. She's the last to get ready. All nine of us bridesmaids have had our make-up and our hair done. My skin is caked with foundation and my eyelids are heavy with false lashes. I feel like one of Ru Paul's drag queens.

Now Scarlett's having her make-up done. But midway, she says, "I feel sick!" and rushes off to the en-suite bathroom. We hear noisy retching through the door.

"Oh dear," says Joanne.

"It's nerves," says Tiffany.

"Are you all right in there?" asks the make-up artist.

At last Scarlett emerges. Her face is pale, despite the make-up. Her lipstick is smudged.

"I …" Scarlett starts to say, but Joanne stops her.

"No time for talking now! The ceremony is in thirty minutes! You're not even in your dress yet."

"But …" says Scarlett. Then she sits down. "You're right. I'm fine. Just nervous."

She gets herself together and finishes getting ready. Then we head downstairs to where the ceremony is being held in a big room in the basement of the hotel.

At the far end of the room we can see Adam and his best man, Charlie. Mum and Dad are sitting in the front row. There's Carolyn – dad's first wife – and her husband, Jim. He has twin daughters from his first marriage. The tall, dark-haired man waiting for us at the doorway must be Scarlett's dad. And somewhere in the room will be his wife – the Predatory Librarian – and maybe she has kids too.

There's something nice about the way that a wedding connects all these people. And not just family – it gives all of Scarlett's and Adam's friends a chance to come together and celebrate. And maybe that's why we all get dressed up for weddings. Maybe it's because we normally don't celebrate together, so we want to look like very glamorous versions of ourselves.

The theme song from *Titanic* starts playing and we're about to walk down the aisle towards Adam when I realise my sandal strap has come undone. I bend down to buckle it, and ... there's an awful ripping noise ...

"Oh my god!" says Tiffany.

I straighten up. I try to twist round to see the damage.

"I can see your knickers!" Tiff hisses.

OH NOOOOOOOOOOOO ...

Chapter 21

"Emergency!" says Tiffany. She grabs my hand and pulls me into a corner. "Don't panic. I'm prepared for anything."

"I can't be a bridesmaid like this!" I say, panting with panic.

"Come on, girls," calls Amisha. "We're on!"

I feel Tiffany grab my dress and pull the fabric together. "There ..." she says. "That should work. And after the ceremony you can change into your amazing peacock dress."

"What have you done?" I ask her.

"Safety pins!" Tiff explains. "My Textiles teacher says you should always have them on you in case of a disaster. I pinned them to my sash," she adds proudly.

"Tiffany, you are amazing," I say.

We join the parade of bridesmaids.

Scarlett takes her dad's arm. "You look so beautiful," he tells her.

"Thanks, Daddy!" Scarlett replies.

"Now, before we do this, are you totally certain?" her dad asks. "This is your chance to say no, if you're not."

Oh no! Scarlett turns pale. "Totally certain?" she says. "I don't think I'm ever totally certain about anything." She's pale as a ghost. "I think ... I might be about to faint."

"Stop the music!" someone calls.

There's a buzz of noise among the guests, and I can see Adam's worried face. Someone finds a chair for Scarlett and pushes her head down between her knees.

"The problem is that Scarlett's never sure about anything," Tiffany whispers to me. "She never has been. It's amazing that she ever said yes to Adam in the first place."

"I'm not sure ... I can't do this ..." says Scarlett's faint voice.

And suddenly I know what I have to do.

I forget being nervous.

I forget to worry about people looking at me.

I forget that there's a strong danger of my knickers being on show, despite Tiffany's best efforts.

I forget that I'm wearing silly silver sandals designed with no thought for health and safety.

I march up to the front of the room, to where Adam's standing with his best man and the registrar (who is looking at her watch).

The guests erupt into oohs and aahs and some giggles. From the cold breeze I can feel on my nether regions, I'm guessing that Tiffany's safety pins didn't all make it on my journey.

Never mind. I'm on a mission. I grip Adam's arm.

"Adam, Scarlett is feeling really nervous," I say. "You have to go and talk to her now."

He's pale too. "Is she OK?" Adam asks.

"Just nervous, I think. Go and talk to her." I reach up to hug him and there's a gasp from the audience. I guess the last of the safety pins has given way. "It'll be OK. She loves you. It's just that the whole fuss and bother is too much for her. At least, that's what I think. You've got this."

Adam kisses the top of my head and says, "Thanks, Miri." And then he hurries off, and I find a chair to sit down on.

"Do you think it'll be sorted out soon?" the registrar asks. "It's just that I've got another wedding in half an hour."

"I just don't know," I say. "It could be yes – and I hope so. But it might be no."

Chapter 22

We wait and wait and wait.

Joanne breaks down in tears.

The Predatory Librarian says, "She needs a stiff drink," and goes to fetch Joanne a whisky. And then a lot of people decide they need a stiff drink too.

Sophie and Tiffany ask various guests if they can borrow their pashminas. Then they cleverly knot them round my thighs and bum. The cold breeze doesn't bother me any more. Tiffany is very apologetic for the safety-pin fail.

Adam's best man, Charlie, turns out to be an amateur magician, so he does some tricks to keep everyone entertained.

The registrar says, "I'm terribly sorry, but I can't wait any longer. People always think their wedding is the only one happening that day, but I'm afraid that's not true. I've got another three couples to marry today. Good luck to you all, and maybe I'll see you all again someday soon."

A while later, the hotel manager suggests that we all move upstairs to the banqueting hall because the catering staff are ready to serve our meal.

Just as everyone has sat down, Adam and Scarlett reappear. In jeans. But holding hands.

The room goes silent.

Adam says, "I'm sorry, everyone. It turns out we weren't ready to get married today. The big day was just ... too big."

"It's all my fault," says Scarlett. "I needed to be sure that I wasn't just doing it for the dress and the fuss and ... oh, everything."

"But we still really love each other," Adam adds.

"Yes, we do," Scarlett says.

"And we want you to have a good time."

"Yes, that's right."

"And we'll just carry on with the rest of our lives," Adam says. "And maybe one day Scarlett and I will get married. But if we do, don't worry, we'll do it on a beach somewhere."

"And if you want to take your presents back, then that's fine of course," Scarlett says.

"But we thought we would give living together a go first."

"Because I can't imagine anyone I'd rather live with than Adam."

"And I'm completely mad about Scarlett."

The whole room of people had been holding their breath, but now everyone breathes again – and claps. The band starts playing, and we might as well be at a wedding.

Apart from Joanne, who's crying in a corner, with Tiffany holding her hand. I catch Tiffany's eye, and she winces. Reluctantly I go and see if I can help.

"I'm just ... humiliated," Joanne says.

"No, Mum, you really aren't," Tiff says.

"What will everyone think?" Joanne asks.

"They'll probably just think that Scarlett didn't want to rush into getting married," I say, but that doesn't seem to help.

"I just wanted a perfect day," says Joanne. "Because my wedding day was perfect. And while things went wrong afterwards, I always had that day to look back on."

"Sure," says Tiffany. "But it's better to have a great life than one perfect day. Isn't it? Just statistically speaking?"

"Oh, Tiff, you know I'm no good at Maths," Joanne says.

"No, Mum, but I am," Tiffany replies. "And actually, I never want to get married. I want to do a Maths degree and then train as a pilot."

Joanne takes a gulp of her whisky. Then she says, "Well, at least you'd get discount air tickets. I take it you're not thinking of the RAF?"

"I haven't made my mind up yet," Tiff says.

Joanne sniffs. "As long as you're happy," she says. "That's what matters. And travelling the world, who knows who you'll meet?"

Then Ronaldo, the personal trainer, comes to ask Joanne to dance.

"Go on, Mum," says Tiffany.

"Oh well. If you insist," says Joanne. "At least I look better than the Predatory Librarian. Don't I, Tiff?"

Tiffany waits until she's gone and then says, "Parents are a bit of a worry."

"So are siblings," I say. "But I think we've sorted them out."

Then I go and get changed into my amazing peacock dress, and we take a whole load of selfies with Sophie. And we dance and eat and laugh.

And then Adam makes a speech, saying thank you to everyone for being so understanding.

"And thank you to Miri," Adam adds. "My little sister. She told me to go and talk to Scarlett at just the right minute."

"Yes, thank you, Miri," says Scarlett.

And then everyone is clapping and shouting, "Speech, speech!"

Adam says, "Go on, Miri."

I really don't want to. I still hate everyone looking at me. But I remember the speeches at Jacob and Alice's wedding, and I feel a bit bad for Adam and Scarlett if no one says anything about them as a couple.

So I say, "Well, now that I'm a very experienced bridesmaid, I know that not everyone needs to get married to live really happy lives.

"Like my mum and dad – they are a great example of a couple who are totally fine without ever having had a wedding.

"And I can tell you, Scarlett, that Adam's more than just a tall, handsome, successful banker.

"He chooses the best birthday presents. He helps me with the most impossible Maths homework. And until very recently he used to let me plait his hair.

"So, you know, he's worth getting to know even better. And I don't know you very well, but any sister of my friend Tiffany is a friend of mine.

"Umm. So." I pause. I can't think of what else to say. Then I catch Jacob's eye, and he raises his glass. I remember how people drank toasts at his and Alice's wedding.

"So please, everyone, raise your glasses and drink a toast," I say. "They might not have got married, but we still love them. To Adam and Scarlett!"

Later on, I'm dancing with my dad. He says, "I can't believe the change in you. Six months ago, would you have had the confidence to get up in front of a roomful of people and make a speech like that?"

"Of course not," I say.

"What made all the difference?" Dad asks.

"Lots of things," I tell him. "Boxing ... and friends ... and the theatre thing ... and the right dress ..."

"So you're a happier Miri now?"

"Yes!" I say. "Yes, I totally am!"

"That's great news," Dad says. "Because your mum and I ... we think it's time to get married ourselves. Fifteen years together – we've waited long enough."

Oh!

"So will you be our bridesmaid?" Dad asks.

No, I think. *Here we go again.*

But then I look around. I see Alice dancing with Jacob, and Mum chatting to Carolyn, and the Predatory Librarian demonstrating Scottish country dancing to Tiffany and Sophie. And I think weddings are pretty fun really – even non-weddings. And maybe I can ask Julie to make me another dress.

So I give Dad a big hug and I say, "Yes! I'd love to be your bridesmaid. Bring it on!"

Our books are tested
for children and young people by
children and young people.

Thanks to everyone who consulted on
a manuscript for their time and effort in
helping us to make our books better
for our readers.